Mayer, Mercer

A boy, a dog, a
frog and a friend

$8.89

DATE			
JY 06 '88			
MY 15 '89	AG 3 '93		
JE 28 '89	OCT 26 '96		
JY 17 '89	FEB 22 '96		
JY 16 '90	AUG 28 '96		
SE 27 '90	NOV 30 '96		
NO 13 '90	DEC 20 '96		
JE 24 '92	[illegible]		
MY 28 '93	[illegible]		
JY [illegible] '93	[illegible]		

A BOY, A DOG, A FROG and A FRIEND

by Mercer

and Marianna Mayer

DIAL BOOKS FOR YOUNG READERS
New York

Published by Dial Books for Young Readers
A division of E. P. Dutton | A division of New American Library
2 Park Avenue, New York, New York 10016

Library of Congress Catalog Card Number: 70-134857
Printed in Hong Kong by South China Printing Co.
COBE
10 12 14 15 13 11

For crazy Dina